inspired by the true story of Hope

Dolphin Tale 2™

A Tale of Winter and Hope

Adapted by Gabrielle Reyes

Based upon the screenplay written by Charles Martin Smith

SCHOLASTIC INC.

ISBN 978-0-545-68175-9

Reader cover design Erin McMahon.
Published by Scholastic Inc.

10 9 8 7 6 5 4 3   14 15 16 17 18 19/0
Printed in the U.S.A.   40

It was a sunny day in Florida when a little girl found a bottlenose dolphin stuck in a muddy lagoon. The dolphin needed help! The Clearwater Marine Aquarium staff arrived quickly.

Sawyer Nelson, a teenage boy who worked for CMA, ran down to the beach to help the other staff members.

Sawyer and his friends took the dolphin back to the aquarium's medical pools and named her Mandy. Mandy had a lung infection and a bad sunburn. The team gave Mandy medicine and put a special lotion on her sunburned skin.

One afternoon, Sawyer and his best friend Hazel were working with the aquarium's other dolphins, Winter and Panama.

Winter was the first dolphin Sawyer had ever rescued. Four years earlier, he had found Winter on the beach with her tail caught in a crab trap. When he called for help, a team from the Clearwater Marine Aquarium came to the rescue.

Winter's tail was so damaged that the CMA team couldn't save it. But Sawyer had a great idea. He asked a special doctor to make a plastic tail for her. Winter got used to her new tail, and had been healthy and happy ever since.

Panama had lived at CMA for a long time,
and she was much older than Winter. But that
didn't stop the two dolphins from living in the
same pool and being best friends.

One day, while Sawyer worked with Winter in the pool, she kept splashing him and squealing loudly. Sawyer told Phoebe, one of the marine specialists, that Winter was acting strangely.

Phoebe said Panama was acting strangely, too, and that she hadn't eaten anything all day. She and Sawyer started to worry.

When Sawyer got to the aquarium the next day, he knew something was wrong. Dr. Clay, the head of the aquarium and Hazel's father, told Sawyer the bad news: Panama had passed away in the night.

Everyone was sad but no one was as upset as Winter. Without Panama, Winter was alone in the dolphin pools. Dolphins need to be around other dolphins or else they get sad and sick. Dr. Clay explained to Sawyer and Hazel that if they didn't move another dolphin into the pool with Winter, she would have to go to another aquarium.

Sawyer and Hazel didn't understand. Mandy was in the medical pools and getting better every day. *Why didn't Dr. Clay just put Mandy in the pool with Winter?* Dr. Clay explained that Mandy might be healthy enough to go back to the ocean. The goal of CMA was to rescue, rehabilitate, and release animals when possible.

If Mandy could survive in the wild, it wouldn't be fair to keep her at the aquarium.

Hazel was angry with her father. She thought he wasn't doing enough to keep Winter. But after she studied Mandy's medical files, she knew he was right. Dr. Clay let Hazel run Mandy's last test to see if she was ready to go back to the ocean.

Hazel told Phoebe to throw three live fish into the pool. As soon as Mandy saw the fish, she whipped around. *Whap-whap-whap!* She caught all three fish in no time.

Watching Mandy zoom around, Hazel and Sawyer could see what was best for her. She was fully recovered and belonged back in the ocean.

On the morning of Mandy's release, there was a lot to do. Hazel, Sawyer, Dr. Clay, and the other marine specialists carefully moved Mandy out of the CMA truck and down to the shore.

They waded into the water with Mandy on the stretcher. Hazel stopped to make sure Mandy's transmitter was working. The transmitter would help them track Mandy in the ocean.

Dr. Clay slid Mandy into the cool water. The dolphin rolled onto her back, then onto her front again, getting a feel for the water.

Swiftly, she gave a big flip of her tail. She was off! "Go, Mandy! Go!" everyone cheered.

Sawyer's cousin, Kyle, watched Mandy's transmitter signal from a boat far from shore. On his GPS, he could see that she was swimming toward a large group of . . . something.

Kyle and the rest of the team were afraid for Mandy. Was she heading for a school of sharks?

SPLASH! Suddenly, Mandy leapt up out of the water followed by another dolphin . . . then another . . . then another! Mandy had found her family, and they were welcoming her home.

A few days later, Dr. Clay was in his office, feeling miserable. He kept thinking about Winter. He worried that he had made the wrong decision letting Mandy go. Now the aquarium would lose Winter. Just then, his phone rang. Harbor Marine Rescue had found a stranded dolphin on the beach!

Dr. Clay called the team right away. Everyone rushed to the aquarium to get ready for the dolphin.

When the rescue truck arrived at CMA, the staff was shocked to see that the dolphin was a tiny, young female.

She was so little, they didn't know if she would survive. So Hazel decided to name her Hope.

Hope was small but strong. Everyone was thrilled to see how quickly she got better. But because she was so young, she didn't know how to catch fish in the wild. She couldn't go back to the ocean.

The young dolphin lived up to her name in more ways than one. She was everything that Sawyer and Hazel were hoping for.

Hope could stay at CMA, which meant that Winter could, too. It didn't take long before Winter and Hope became the best of friends.

About the real-life Mandy, Winter, and Hope

Mandy was last seen healthy and happy in the Gulf of Mexico.

The team at CMA continues to work on Winter's tail as improvements in technology develop.

Winter and Hope are thriving at CMA and continue to inspire millions around the world. They can be seen at CMA or online at Seewinter.com.